Contents

For Faith

The Forgotten Puppy

The Forgotten Puppy

by Holly Webb

Illustrated by Sophy Williams

tiger tales

5 River Road, Suite 128, Wilton, CT 06897
Published in the United States 2018
Originally published in Great Britain 2007
by the Little Tiger Group
Text copyright © 2007 Holly Webb
Illustrations copyright © 2007 Sophy Williams
ISBN-13: 978-1-68010-430-1
ISBN-10: 1-68010-430-6
Printed in China
STP/1800/0179/0218
10 9 8 7 6 5 4 3 2 1

For more insight and activities, visit us at www.tigertalesbooks.com

Chapter One
An Important Talk

"It looks weird," Emi said, staring anxiously around the empty room.

"Only because there's nothing in it, silly," her older brother, Ben, told her. He had a special older-brother voice he used for saying things like that, and Emi glared at him. Just because he was 14, it didn't mean he knew everything.

"I know that! It just still looks … weird. It doesn't look like our house."

"It will when all our things are in it, Emi, don't worry." Mom was standing in the doorway holding a box. "In a week it'll feel like we've always lived here, I promise. Now, can you two come and help me unload the car? The moving van will be here with the rest of our stuff soon, and I want to get these things into the kitchen first."

After a last worried look around their new living room, Emi followed them out to the car. There was one good thing about this house, she realized, and her eyes brightened a little. Through the window, she could see out into a yard. That had been one of the things that made them all love the place. The yard wasn't huge, and it was a little messy—Mom said all those straggly bushes needed a trim—but at least it was there. The apartment that they'd been living in since Mom and Dad had decided to split up didn't have a yard at all—just a little concrete area for the garbage cans.

Emi hurried after Mom and Ben, smiling to herself. She couldn't wait to unpack—getting out her clothes and books would make the bedroom feel like it was really hers. For the last couple of weeks, everything had been in boxes. She wasn't actually sure where anything was, but discovering things again would be part of the fun. She hadn't seen her favorite purple sweater or her slippers for what seemed like forever.

And once they were all completely unpacked—settled, Mom called it— then they could start to think about the most important part of the move. It was the most important part for Emi, anyway.

Now that they had a yard, Mom had said that at last, after years of *maybe* and *one day* and *when you're older*, they could get a dog.

"Mom…."

"Mm-hm?"

"Mom, are you actually listening? You look like you're thinking about whether that picture is in the wrong place. Again."

It had been five weeks since they'd moved in, and Emi's mom was still worrying about whether everything was in the right spot or not. She blinked and looked at Emi guiltily.

"You're right, I was. I'm sorry. It just doesn't seem to fit there, and it's getting to me. I really am listening now."

"Except for that picture and not liking the shape of the bath faucets and

11

the way that cupboard door squeaks in the kitchen—" Emi was counting on her fingers—"do you think we're almost settled in?"

Her mom smiled at her. "I suppose so. Do you feel like we are?"

"Yes!" Emi looked at her pleadingly. "Do you remember—you said that when we were settled, we could think about getting a dog. I don't mean we should actually get one right this minute, but we could at least think about it, couldn't we? What kind of dog we'd like and where we'd get it from? Please?"

Her mom nodded. "I hadn't forgotten, Emi. I've been thinking about it, too. Go and see if Ben is finished with that homework he was doing and ask him to come down here for a minute."

Emi raced up the stairs. She was pretty sure that Ben wasn't doing his homework at all—she could hear him talking to one of his friends about the computer game they were playing, but by the time she got upstairs and banged on his door, he had his English essay up on the screen and was looking all innocent.

"What, Emi? I'm working."

It was tempting to point out that he'd only written about three lines, but the last thing Emi wanted was to get into an argument with her older brother. That would be an absolutely perfect way to make Mom forget about getting a dog.

13

"Mom wants to talk to us. About the dog! Can you come down, pleeease?"

Ben yanked off his headphones and jumped up. He was almost as excited about having a dog as Emi was, especially since he was old enough to remember Akiko, the dog Mom and Dad had owned years ago. Akiko had died when Emi was really young, and she didn't remember him at all.

Emi hurried back down to the living room, with Ben jumping down the stairs after her. When she got there, the little table in front of the couch was covered in old photograph albums. She glared at her mom. "You said we could talk about dogs!" she cried out. "You're not supposed to be unpacking more stuff!"

Her mom laughed. "I'm not. I was trying to find some pictures that I wanted to show you. Look—do you see who that is?"

Emi and Ben stared down at the photo in the album—a little girl with a very serious face and dark hair cut in a fringe. Emi thought the girl looked like her, but she didn't remember ever wearing jeans like that....

"It's you, Mom, isn't it?" Ben said. "Was that in Japan?"

"Yes." Mom nodded. "I must have been about six there, I think."

Emi looked at the photo curiously. Mom didn't talk that much about her life in Japan. She'd come to the United States as a student, and then she'd met Dad, and she hadn't been back all that often. Their Japanese grandparents— Emi and Ben called them *Sobo* and *Sofu*, which meant Grandma and Grandpa in Japanese—sent them presents on their birthdays and at Christmas and they called every few weeks, but Emi had only met them once, when they'd come over to visit a couple of years ago.

"This is the one I wanted you to see." Mom turned the page and showed them the same little girl—she even had the same jeans on—but this time, she was sitting next to a dog with her arm around its neck. Both of them looked so happy that Emi couldn't help saying, "Awwww...."

Ben rolled his eyes at her. "You never told us you had a dog when you were little, Mom!"

"So cute.... But what type of dog is that?" Emi asked, frowning. She was usually excellent at naming dog breeds. She had a poster on her wall that had come with one of Dad's newspapers, showing all kinds of different dogs. But she wasn't sure about this one at all.

"Actually, are you sure that isn't a fox?" Ben asked, peering at the little photo. "It has a real fox face with those pointy ears! And a bushy tail."

"No, it's fatter than a fox," Emi said thoughtfully. "I know what you mean, though, and it's even fox-colored—kind of golden-red."

Mom laughed. "He wasn't a fox. He was a Shiba Inu. They're a Japanese breed. And he was named Kin—

that means gold." She smiled down at the picture. "He was the best. The friendliest dog ever. He used to follow me around when I was little, almost like a babysitter. He'd bark at Sobo to tell her if I was crawling too far away, and she'd come and pick me up."

"He's beautiful. He looks like he's smiling. What does Shiba Inu mean in Japanese, Mom?" Emi only knew a few words of her mom's native language, like her name and Ben's. Her brother was actually named Benjiro, which meant peaceful (Emi thought Mom and Dad had picked pretty badly with that one). But he was always just Ben, and most people didn't know he had a Japanese name. With Emi it was the other way around. Her full name was Emily, but

Mom always called her Emi. She'd explained that it meant "beautiful gift." She and Dad had wanted their children to have names that worked in both languages. Emi liked it—it felt special to have two names.

"Inu just means dog," Mom said. "The Shiba part isn't so clear, though. There's a kind of tree with the same name that turns reddish-gold in the autumn, so that could be it. Or some people think it means small. In one of the old Japanese languages, Shiba means small, and they're very small dogs." She laughed. "Kin only looks big because I was so little...."

"Can you get them in this country?" Emi asked thoughtfully. It would be really cool to have a Japanese dog.

And she liked the idea of taking a dog like that for walks in the park, where people asked each other what breed their dogs were. She always asked the owners if she didn't know—most people loved talking about their dogs.

Mom looked at Emi and Ben. "You know I called Mariko over the weekend?" Mariko had been a friend of Mom's since they were in school together. She was Japanese, too, and came to stay with them sometimes. "Another friend of hers—Kaii—owns a rescue center that's just for Shiba Inus. She was telling me that it's not very far from here. In fact, he has a litter of puppies right now...."

Ben grinned. "Mom! Do you mean we could have one?"

Emi was much too excited to say anything—she just gave Mom the most enormous hug.

Chapter Two
Meeting the Puppies

"A Shiba Inu?" Emi's best friend, Kyla, shook her head as they walked through the school playground. "I don't think I've ever heard of them! What do they look like?"

"Really, really beautiful...," Emi sighed happily. "They're not very big, but they're sort of solid-looking, if you know what I mean? Chunky, I guess.

Ben said Mom's old dog looked like a fox, because they have pointy faces and hers was an orange-red color. But you can get black and tan Shiba Inus, too, and even white ones." She giggled. "Mom showed us some photos online, and there was a white Shiba Inu puppy—he looked like a snowball with ears. Their fur isn't really fluffy, but it sticks out a bit, and he was so roly-poly and cute...."

Kyla laughed. "You've fallen in love, Emi!" Then she shivered. "Ooooh, speaking of snowballs, I wish the bell would ring. I'm frozen. I wouldn't be surprised if it actually snowed soon. I really wanted us to have a white Christmas, but all it did was rain over the vacation...."

"Maybe we'll get a snow day instead—that would be good. Imagine playing with a puppy in the snow...." Emi couldn't think of anything better.

"So, do you know when you're going to get the puppy?" asked Kyla. "And can I come over to see it? Please?"

Emi put an arm around her friend's shoulders. "Of course you can! But I don't think we'll be getting the puppy for a little while. Mom called the friend of her friend who works at the rescue center, though, and we're going to go and visit one weekend.  Mom said it would be too tricky to fit it in after school. And this weekend we can't, because we're going to Dad's. We're seeing his new apartment for the first time. You know he moved, too, right?"

Kyla nodded. Her parents didn't live together, either—it was one of the things that she and Emi had in common—that and the fact that they both loved animals. Kyla had three cats at her dad's house and guinea pigs at her mom and stepdad's. They both understood what it was like having two families and two houses. Kyla knew all about having to remember which house you'd left your homework at and sometimes forgetting which family was picking you up from school.

"Mom said none of the puppies could come home with us for a few weeks anyway," Emi explained. "They have to be at least eight weeks old before they can leave their mother, and they aren't quite that big yet. Almost, though!"

"When you get the puppy, will you be able to take him to your dad's, too?" Kyla asked thoughtfully.

Emi shook her head slowly. "I don't think so. It's a pretty tiny apartment. Dad's going to have to sleep on the couch while we're staying so we'll all fit. And we're going to take a train to get there. Dad can come straight from work to meet us at the station. It's not far from the apartment, he says. If he drove to pick us up at our house, we wouldn't get there until really late. I'm not sure a puppy would like going on a train very much."

"You're going on a train on your own?" Kyla sounded envious.

"With Ben." Emi sighed. "He's going to be a nightmare. Mom and Dad keep saying he has to take care of me, so it's like the ultimate excuse for him to be a bossy big brother. 'I'm in charge, you've got to do as I say, you're only nine, blah blah blah....'"

Kyla giggled, and Emi grinned at her. "Well, he *is* like that!"

🐾 🐾 🐾 🐾

Emi stood between Mom and Ben on the doorstep of Kaii's rescue center. She was feeling a strange mixture of excited and sad—they were going to meet their new puppy for the first time, so of course

28

she was excited! But she wished Dad was with them. It had been wonderful going to see his new apartment last weekend. She'd really missed him when they hadn't seen him for a few weeks because of his move. Dad had played computer games with them, and he'd brought them out to the woods near his new apartment, and even though Ben had said walks were boring, it had been really fun. They'd run around and jumped over a stream. Emi had almost fallen in, but Dad had caught her just in time.

There was a little wooded area near their new house, too, Emi remembered, as she listened to the sound of barking on the other side of the door. They'd be able to take their new puppy on walks there soon!

Maybe Dad would get a pet, too, she thought, as Mom smiled down at her. But not a dog—not when he was at work all day. They were really lucky that Mom mostly worked from home, so they wouldn't be leaving their new puppy alone too much.

"Hello! Erika, yes? And Emi and Ben? I'm Kaii." He beamed at them as he opened the door. His sweater was covered in dog hair, but Emi was hardly looking at him because peering nosily around his legs were two beautiful dogs. The larger dog was black and tan, but the smaller one was the same golden-red color as Kin, her mom's old dog. Seeing the Shiba Inu breed for real, instead of in a faded photo, Emi realized that they were so much more beautiful. Their pointed, pricked-up ears made them look really smart. They had whitish fur around their dark eyes, too, which made them stand out. Both of the dogs were staring at Emi now, with their heads to one side, as though they were trying to figure out what they thought of her.

Kaii was laughing, Emi suddenly realized, and so were Mom and Ben. Emi looked up at them, her face turning red. What had she done?

"It's okay," Kaii said, smiling. "I was just saying that you all should come in! I don't think you heard a word I said, though. You like them, then?"

"They're *beautiful*!" Emi told him as they followed him inside. She'd love to have a puppy that grew up like these two. She was sure they were grinning at her as well. One of them had his tongue hanging out. "And they look really smart."

"They are," he agreed. "And they make good pets, too. They're very loving. But you do have to be firm with them, or they walk all over you."

"What are their names?" Emi asked.

"This is Daisuke, and this is Kimi," said Kaii. "They both arrived here as strays. The puppies are in the puppy room at the moment. Would you like something to drink first?"

Emi looked at her mom hopefully, and Mom smiled and shook her head. "No, that's okay. Thank you, though! Emi's so desperate to see the puppies that I think she might explode if I say yes."

"Come on, then," Kaii said as he led them through the house. "I have a room for the puppies at the back of the center—it leads into the yard, so they can go outside when they're big enough…. Here we are. Just come in quietly to start with, so you don't startle them—they're very friendly, but we have to let them get used to you."

Emi and Ben practically tiptoed into the room. In one corner, curled up asleep in the big basket, were four round, furry puppies, fast asleep.

"Don't worry. They'll wake up in a minute," Kaii told them as he watched Ben and Emi trying to peer over and get a good look at the pile of puppies. "They have a sixth sense—they always know when something interesting is happening. See? I told you!"

One of the puppies, who was black and tan, had popped his head up so quickly that Emi couldn't help laughing. "He looks like a teddy bear," she whispered to Ben, and her brother grinned. It was the way the fur stood up all around their heads and paws, Emi decided. As the puppy climbed over his brothers and sisters to come and investigate, he looked like too much of a fluffball to be real.

The other puppies squeaked angrily and woke up as he stomped over them, and then Emi gasped. There weren't four puppies—there were five! Now that they were all moving, she could see another puppy who'd been snuggled up at the bottom of the heap, with the others on top. And this puppy was a beautiful golden color.

"Look...." She nudged her mom.

"I know, they're so cute," Mom whispered back. "Oh, look, they're all waking up now. They're coming to see us!" She reached out, and one of the creamy-white puppies sniffed her fingers curiously and then licked her.

The golden puppy let out a big yawn and scratched its front paws against the blanket.

"That tail looks like a little doughnut, curled up like that. Is the golden puppy a girl?" Emi asked Kaii. "She looks like a girl...."

"Yes! Very good. She's quite pretty, isn't she?"

Pretty! Emi wanted to tell him that the puppy was the most beautiful dog she'd ever seen, but she didn't want everyone to laugh at her again.

The golden puppy stumbled out of the basket and came to see what her brothers and sisters were looking at. There were new, interesting smells.... Exciting smells! She trotted across the room and sniffed at Emi's boots. Then she looked up with dark, sparkling eyes and put her fluffy little paw softly on Emi's leg, as if she was saying, *You belong to me....*

Chapter Three
Making Friends

"What will you name her?" Kyla asked with a little sigh. "You're so lucky, getting a puppy!"

"We're not sure yet," Emi told her. "We keep arguing about it—it's really difficult to choose. But I like one of the names Mom suggested, Miki. It's pretty just by itself, and it means beautiful in Japanese."

Kyla nodded. "That's so nice! Oh, look, there's your mom. E-mail me a picture of her, Emi! Have a good weekend."

Emi waved as she dashed off to meet her mom at the school gate. First they were going to meet Ben (around the corner from his school, though, as he said it was much too embarrassing to be picked up by his mom and little sister), and then they were driving over to the rescue center to bring their puppy home. There was a special new metal crate in the back of the car for the puppy to travel in, and at home there was a basket and food bowls and a bunch of toys.

When Kaii had come over from the rescue center earlier in the week to check that the house was safe enough for Miki and it was all confirmed they could definitely get the little golden puppy, they'd gone shopping. Emi had darted excitedly around the pet store, choosing everything the puppy could possibly need and more. Mom had persuaded her to put most of it back, though—the puppy didn't need three leashes, after all. Emi knew that, really. It was just so much fun picking out the different things and imagining the puppy using them and drinking from her new water bowl and playing with all the toys.

Ben had said he thought Emi was so excited that she was going to try sleeping in the puppy's basket, but that was just Ben being silly. She had rubbed the furry cushion in it, that was all, and tried to think of a little golden puppy sleeping there, all curled up. The basket was going to be huge for the puppy at first.

"Come on, Mom, let's go!" Emi raced down the road, pulling her mom after her. "Ben had better be quick getting out of school...."

But Ben was already waiting for them, and he looked impatient, too.

Emi sat in the back of the car, staring dreamily out the window. She wasn't seeing the streets they drove past at all—she was imagining walks with their puppy and sitting curled up together on the couch. Or maybe on the floor. Mom wasn't sure about dogs on furniture, but Emi was hoping she'd give in after a while....

The golden puppy heard the doorbell ring and jumped up. She knew by now what that noise meant. Voices at the door and then quite often people coming to see her and her brothers and sisters, and play with them. She liked that—most of the time. Some of the people scared her—they were too loud and picked her up too suddenly. She padded to the door and sniffed at it hopefully. The day before, one of her brothers had gone away with the people who'd come to visit. She missed him. It had been strange, curling up in the big basket without him last night. She wondered if maybe this would be the people bringing him back.

But when Kaii carefully opened the door, the golden puppy saw the girl again—the one she remembered from a short time ago. She had snuggled into that girl's lap, she was sure. The girl had rubbed her ears and whispered to her. There had been a boy, too, and he'd thrown a jingly ball for her to play with. He wasn't quite as warm and cuddly as the girl, but she'd liked him, too.

She danced up to Emi and Ben, yapping excitedly and wagging her little curl of a tail.

Emi looked at Kaii hopefully. "Do you think she remembers us?"

Kaii was smiling. "I think so. She hasn't been that friendly to any of the other visitors. She's been a little quiet today, actually. I think she's missing her brother. He went to a new home yesterday."

"Ohhh…." Emi crouched down to pet the puppy. "I hadn't thought about that. You're going to miss all your brothers and sisters when you come home with us…."

The puppy leaned into Emi's hand, closing her eyes blissfully. It was definitely the same girl. She knew just how to rub her ears. The puppy leaned in a little more and then her claws skittered and scratched on the tiled floor, and she flipped over.

The puppy stood up, shaking her ears and looking bewildered. She wasn't exactly sure what had happened. But the girl reached down gently and picked her up, holding her close.

"Oh, look at her," Mom laughed. "She's all fluffed up and worried. She's so cute. I really do think she looks like a Sweetie."

Ben nodded. "Maybe. But I'm not shouting 'Sweetie' in the middle of the park. Let's go with Miki."

"I can't believe we're bringing you home and we got to choose your name," Emi whispered into Miki's furry ear. "We'll take care of you so well, I promise."

Emi was glad they'd gone to get Miki on a Friday night and now they had the entire weekend to get to know her. Kaii had suggested that it would be best to keep her in the kitchen at first, so she wasn't too scared by the big, strange house. But Emi was pretty sure Miki wasn't scared of anything.

Ben put her down on the kitchen floor when they first got home, and she went marching around the room on her little stubby legs, inspecting everything carefully. She stood by the glass back door and barked at a very surprised pigeon, and then they saw her tail wag for the first time. Because it was curled up so tightly over her back, she didn't wag it the same way most dogs did. It just wobbled instead.

"Look at her tail!" Emi laughed. "It looks like a caterpillar wriggling!"

"That pigeon got a shock." Ben peered out into the yard. "I think it might be up in the apple tree panicking now."

But Miki looked very pleased with herself. She went back to exploring the kitchen, sniffing at her bed and all her new toys, and looking hopefully at her food bowl. She knew what that was.

"Yes, we'd better feed you," Mom

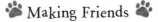

told her, and Miki danced up and down excitedly as she saw Mom opening the bag. After she'd gobbled down the food, she flopped into her new basket. It was too big for her—she looked a little lost in the middle of it. She sniffed all around it worriedly and then looked up at Emi, Ben, and Mom.

"I think she's wondering where the other puppies are," Emi said anxiously.

"Maybe," her mom agreed.

"I've got an idea," Emi said suddenly, rushing out of the kitchen. She shut the door carefully behind her and hurried up the stairs. She was back down a minute later with a huge teddy bear that she'd won at the school fair several years ago. It had dark-gold fur, and it was incredibly soft. Emi laid the teddy bear down in the basket next to Miki, and the puppy sniffed at it suspiciously. Then she climbed onto it, rather slowly, as she was very full of food, and slumped down, with her head pillowed on its round, furry middle.

Emi smiled to herself. The puppy was already fast asleep.

Chapter Four
Going Away

"I'm sorry, Miki." Emi sighed and looked down at the puppy, who was nosing at her big backpack. "You can't come, sweetheart." She put the T-shirts she was carrying into the bag and crouched down to hug the little golden dog. "I really wish you could. I'm going to miss you so much." It was the following weekend, and she and Ben were going to stay at their dad's. She glanced around the room. "Have I forgotten anything? Oh! Toothbrush!"

She darted into the bathroom, and Miki galloped after her. The puppy had only stayed in the kitchen for a couple of days—it was clear that she wasn't worried about her new home at all, even if she did miss the other puppies, especially at night.

The big teddy bear helped, though. Miki had moaned and whimpered for a little while when they had left her in the kitchen that first evening. Emi and Mom and Ben had all sat on the stairs listening to her and worrying. She had sounded so sad that Emi had almost cried. Then Miki had stopped, all at once, and there was no more noise until five thirty the next morning. Emi hadn't minded that. She'd gone downstairs in her pajamas as soon as Miki had woken her up—it just meant an even longer day of playing.

Emi thought they might have to buy Miki a new bear soon, though. She'd chewed most of one arm off already. She pulled him around the house with her, too, which was very funny to watch, as the bear was at least twice as big as she was. Emi had filmed her and sent the video to Dad, who said it was the funniest thing he'd ever seen. He was just sorry there was no room for a dog at his apartment.

Miki hadn't brought the bear up to Emi's room, as she had enough trouble just getting herself up the stairs.

They were very steep for a dog with very small legs. She trotted after Emi to the bedroom and peered into the bag again.

She didn't really understand what it was. It looked like Emi's school bag, which was worrying. When Emi had that bag, it meant she was going away and she wouldn't be back until just before dinnertime. But it never seemed to need this much packing. And Emi was sad, Miki could tell. She kept hugging her, but too tightly, almost so hard Miki tried to wriggle away. Something was different.

"Emi, are you ready?" Mom called up. "We need to go—the train leaves in 20 minutes."

"Can we take Miki to the station with us?" Emi begged as she hurried down the stairs to join Ben, with Miki jumping carefully from step to step behind her.

"I guess so," Mom agreed. "It's not far. I can always carry her back."

Emi reached up to get Miki's leash down from the hook, and Miki twirled and danced and yapped in excitement. Emi's mom had taken her for her last vaccinations on Monday, but she'd only had a couple of very short walks since then.

But why wasn't Emi excited, too? When Emi crouched down to clip on her leash, Miki could tell she was still unhappy. She licked Emi's nose, hoping to cheer her up, and Emi giggled, but she didn't sound quite right. She didn't go skipping out into the front yard the way she usually did, either.

Miki stopped, pulling back on her leash as they reached the pavement and whimpering. What was wrong? She didn't want to go out like this.

"Oh!" Emi squatted down next to her. "Do you think Miki can tell we're worried about leaving her behind?"

"Maybe…." Her mom glanced worriedly at her watch. "Maybe we should take her back inside. You'll miss the train."

"No." Emi stood up and tried hard to smile. "It'll be fine. I want her to see us off. Come on, Miki! Let's go!" And she patted her leg encouragingly.

Miki sniffed cautiously at the fence post and then padded out onto the pavement. She wasn't sure what was going on, but Emi and Ben were both coaxing her along, and there were such interesting outside smells....

Emi stared out the window of Dad's apartment, watching an elderly lady walking along the street with her dog. *The dog is elderly, too*, Emi thought, and they were walking at a perfect pace for each other, slow and gentle. She heaved a huge sigh, so huge there was a big misty patch on the glass. She missed Miki so much. She couldn't help thinking about her all the time.

She wasn't sure if she wanted Miki to miss her or not. She didn't want the puppy to be sad, but at the same time, it would be nice to know that Miki cared enough to notice if she wasn't there. When they'd gotten on the train, she had heard Miki howling on the platform next to Mom. She'd done the same thing the first few mornings when they'd left her to go to school. Mom called it her Shiba scream—she said that Shiba Inus were famous for it—and it really did sound like Miki was screaming.

"Are you okay, Emi?" Dad came and sat on the couch next to her. "You look a little sad. Too much homework?"

"It's all done. I'm sorry, Dad. I'm just missing Miki."

Dad hugged her. "You don't have to be sorry. It's hard to leave her behind when you've only had her a week. You can call your mom later to find out how she is."

But all the same, Emi felt guilty for saying it. She didn't want her dad to think she didn't want to see him—she missed him a lot, too. It was just so difficult. She felt like she couldn't ever be in the right place....

🐾 🐾 🐾 🐾

"Ben, look! There's Mom. I can see her. And Miki, too!" Emi bounced up out of her seat, hurrying to the train doors.

"Leaving your bag on the train, are you?" Ben sighed, picking it up and following her, but Emi was hardly listening. The train was pulling in slowly now, and she could see that Mom had picked Miki up to keep her from being scared. She was making Miki wave her paw to them.

Emi giggled and waited impatiently for the doors to open.

"Mom! You brought her!" Emi gasped as she jumped out. "Hello, beautiful Miki! And you, too, Mom," she added quickly, kissing her mom on the cheek.

"Did you miss me at all?" Mom asked, but Emi knew she was only teasing.

"How was Miki after we talked? Did she notice us being away?"

"She definitely did." Mom put Miki down carefully, now that the train was pulling out, and passed Emi the leash.

"She's been really quiet the entire weekend. I'm sure she was waiting for you to come home."

"Oh, poor Miki," Emi sighed.

Ben crouched down to rub the little puppy's ears gently. "We missed you, too," he told her.

"I was glad she was there, though," Mom said, putting an arm around Emi as they walked out of the station. "The house didn't feel so empty. And I might have let her snuggle up with me on the couch and watch TV last night...," she added, looking guilty.

"You said we weren't allowed!" Emi told her indignantly.

"I know—but we were both missing you two, and she was so cuddly and warm. It's definitely gotten colder this weekend. I wouldn't be surprised if it snows soon."

Emi looked down at Miki. "You'll love it if it does, Miki. You've got the perfect fur for snow, all thick and soft!"

Miki stood on the back doorstep, watching Emi worriedly. She was dancing around in the white stuff, her boots leaving deep prints.

It had been cold for a while, but the snow just hadn't come, even though everyone at school had been staring out the classroom windows and hoping for it for weeks. Another two weeks had gone by, and Ben and Emi had been on another visit to Dad's, and still there hadn't been any snow. But now, at last, it had fallen overnight, just in time for mid-semester vacation. Emi had woken Miki up with an excited yell from upstairs, and then she'd come racing down in her pajamas and jumped around the kitchen, practically falling over as she tried to get her boots on.

Miki sniffed at the snow. It smelled odd—clean and cold and somehow sharp. She wasn't sure she liked it, even though Emi obviously did. Miki let out a huffy little breath. Emi was hers, and she had to take care of her. She always went outside when Emi did. Cautiously, she put one paw in the snow and then drew it back again at once. Too cold. Too wet.

Emi floundered back across the yard, giggling and shivering. "Don't you like it, Miki? Oh, you have to like it!"

Miki yapped at her angrily, telling her to come in right now. Emi's cheeks were bright red against her black hair, and she looked frozen.

"Look!" Emi scooped up a handful of the white stuff and showed it to Miki. It looked like a big white ball. Miki's ears pricked up at once. She loved to play fetch—she and Emi could chase a ball around all day long. Ben had tried to teach her to play soccer, too, but she wasn't very good at that. The ball was too big, and she usually got so excited chasing it that she'd try to fling herself on top of the ball and then she'd fall over.

"Fetch? Fetch the ball!" Emi hurled it across the yard, and Miki forgot about the strange white stuff and leaped off the step. She'd bounded halfway across the snow-covered grass before she realized she couldn't actually see the snowball anymore.

Emi was doubled over laughing. "Oh, Miki, it's all the way up to your tummy," she giggled.

Miki snorted angrily. But then she decided she didn't mind that much. The white stuff was cold and wet, but the smell was good after all. And she could dig! She scraped at the snow experimentally with her front paws, and it flew everywhere. She sneezed and then she dug and then she chased her tail in the snow and then she dug some more. Yes, she liked this stuff very much....

Chapter Five
Feeling Forgotten

It was perfect timing—snow for the vacation. And there was an entire week off from school! Emi knew she should be happy—and she was, most of the time. Building a snowman and trying to build an igloo (it didn't really work—it just kept collapsing on her head) and going out on Kyla's sled with Miki. It was all wonderful.

But she was spending part of the week at Dad's, and as much as she wanted to see him, she would miss Miki. He'd called her and Ben and told them all about the exciting trips he had planned—there was a science show at the museum, and the shopping center close to him had set up a mini ice rink. Emi loved the sound of that—she'd never been ice-skating. And he said the woods looked amazing in the snow. There were all sorts of fun things to do. Emi was really looking forward to seeing Dad for a little longer than a weekend, too. But it did mean four whole days away from Miki.

Emi had missed her so much the two weekends they had been at Dad's. And she knew that Miki had missed her, too. And Ben, probably, Emi admitted to herself. Miki loved to play rough and tumble roly-poly wrestling games with him, and she liked sitting on his lap and watching him play on his computer. Especially when he was talking to his friends. Ben got them to say hello to her, too, and it made her really confused, hearing the voices saying her name coming out of the laptop.

Emi sighed as she stuffed some more clothes into her bag. Miki would be fine. Mom would take care of her—and it would be nice for Mom to have Miki, because otherwise she'd be lonely while they were away. But still....

"I wish you could come, too," she told Miki, who was sitting next to the backpack, staring at it suspiciously.

Miki knew what the bag meant by now. Emi was going away. Again!

As soon as Emi turned around to get the rest of her stuff out of the dresser, Miki nudged the bag hard with her nose so that it tipped over and the clothes spilled out all over the floor.

"Miki!" Emi looked at her. "Silly! What are you doing?" She crouched down next to the bag and started putting the clothes back inside. But Miki grabbed a pair of jeans in her teeth and pulled them across the room. Then she sat there in the corner with them, looking determined.

"Oh, Miki…," Emi sighed. "Are you trying to stop me from going? I'll miss you, too, I really will. But I have to go and see Dad. Let's go downstairs and get a drink. I'll finish packing later."

Miki followed her out of the room triumphantly, glancing back at the clothes all over the floor. But the bag was still there and the bright curl of her tail sagged a little as she hurried after Emi.

"Are you all packed, Emi?" Mom was smiling, but she looked as though she was trying a bit too hard, Emi thought. She knew Mom missed them when they were away, even though she always said she loved how quiet the house was without Ben, and how she could cook for herself without worrying about Emi saying everything was too spicy.

"I just need to zip up my bag," Emi said, crossing her fingers behind her back. She was packed, or rather she had been. But she'd have to put back all the things that Miki had knocked onto the floor.

Now where had Miki gone? Emi popped her head around the living-room door to see if there was a fluffy ball snoozing on the couch. Mom had given up even saying that Miki wasn't allowed on the furniture—she was too cozy. But the living room was empty. Emi headed up the stairs. Miki was probably with Ben.

Emi hurried around her room, picking up the things that Miki had pulled out of her bag. She was a little worried about how it was all going to fit back in. It still looked really full. But her things had gone in before....

She knelt beside the bag and pulled it wider open, scooping up a pile of clothes ready to put in. Then she stopped, hugging the sweaters against her as her eyes filled up with tears. That was why the bag was so full. Miki was curled up inside, fast asleep! The puppy had decided that if Emi had to go away again, then this time she was going with her.

Miki stood by the front door, her tail wriggling happily as Emi's mom picked up the leash.

"Not a long walk, though," Mom told her. "It's still freezing cold out there. And really slippery. The snow melted a little yesterday, and now it's frozen over again. Not so good for walking on, Miki. I don't have claws like you, do I?"

Miki nuzzled against Mom's legs. She wanted to go out so much—they hadn't been on as many walks as usual over the last few days. Mom had a lot of work to do, and with Ben and Emi away, it was a good chance to get it done. Miki had spent a lot of the time curled up on Mom's feet in her little office. They had kept each other warm.

Miki sniffed thoughtfully at a pair of Emi's shoes as she waited for

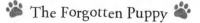

Mom to get her coat on. Where was Emi? Whenever Emi and Ben had gone away before, they'd come back sooner than this, Miki was sure. It felt as though Emi had been away for a very long time. Miki laid her ears back anxiously, almost forgetting the excitement of the walk. Maybe Emi wasn't coming back. Maybe something had happened. What if Emi had forgotten her?

She and Mom had taken Emi and Ben to the train station, just like before, so why hadn't they returned? Maybe they were still at the station, waiting. Miki gave a worried little whine. She wanted Emi back now. It must be time to go and get her. That had to be where they were going.

Her tail started to wriggle again, and her ears pricked forward. She would see Emi soon!

"All right. Let's go." Mom picked up the keys and opened the door. "Just down the road to the park for a bit, okay? Then back for a nice cup of tea. Maybe some dog treats for you."

They set off, with Miki sniffing hopefully along the snowy pavement, wondering if she would come across Emi's scent, or Ben's. At the end of the road, Mom turned left, heading toward the park. But Miki stopped, confused. The train station was the other way. They were going to the station to meet Emi and Ben, weren't they? She tugged on the leash, digging her claws into the snow.

"It's so icy. Don't pull, sweetheart," Mom said. "I don't want to fall. Come on."

Miki shook her ears frantically. Mom was taking them the wrong way. Emi and Ben would be waiting. She and Mom might miss them if they didn't go soon.

She pulled again and let out a questioning whine, but Mom didn't turn back toward the train station.

"No, Miki," she said firmly. "Come on. We're going to the park. Good girl. That's it."

Miki had been going to puppy classes with Mom and Emi, and the trainer had told them how important the tone of voice was for dog training. You have to sound as though you mean it, she'd said. And Kaii had explained to them when they'd first gotten Miki that Shiba Inus could be hard to train if they didn't know that their owners were their pack leaders. Mom had to be top dog, he'd told them. Mom had practiced the firm voice carefully.

So even though Miki didn't want to go down the road to the park, she still did as she was told. She laid her ears back and plodded along like a miserable snail.

But just as they got halfway down the road, Mom slipped on the ice and let go of Miki's leash. Miki sniffed at her carefully and made sure that she was all right. When Mom started to get up, Miki gave her cheek a quick, apologetic, loving lick. And then she darted away, back down the road, before Mom had a chance to catch her breath and call to her.

Chapter Six
An Unexpected Journey

Miki knew the way to the train station really well by now—she had been there several times to drop off and pick up Ben and Emi. So she hurried down the road, her leash trailing over the snow. She could hear Mom behind her, calling her name. She did stop and look back a couple of times. But she knew it was more important to find Emi.

The station seemed different, now that she was here on her own. Had it been this big before, and this busy? There were cars parked all around the entrance, and people talking and hurrying past. Miki tucked herself under a clump of bushes at the edge of the parking lot and peered out at all the feet as they went past. Now that she was actually here, she remembered the thundering growl of the trains, and she wasn't sure she was brave enough to go any farther. She had been scared before, even with Emi and Ben and Mom, and now she was all by herself.

But Emi could be so close! What if Miki missed her because she was huddled up and hiding under a bush? Miki waited for the next pair of feet to go thumping past her and then she stuck her nose out, checking to see if anyone else was coming. The parking lot was quiet. She darted out and followed the man through the gate and past the little ticket office onto the platform.

She couldn't see Emi—but then both times before when Miki and Mom had come to get her, they'd had to wait for a train to pull up and for Emi and Ben to get off. Maybe she needed to wait for a train now. Miki backed carefully underneath one of the benches on the platform and settled down to wait.

After a few minutes, the bench above her began to vibrate, just a little, and Miki realized that a train was coming. She stood up under the bench and stepped forward a little, watching. There were only a few people on the platform, and she could see clearly. Her ears pricked up—she would see Emi soon! And Emi would be so happy, Miki was sure.

The noise grew louder and louder, and then the speaker above Miki's head burst into chattering life as well, making her jump. Miki wriggled back under the bench, shivering, and pressed herself against the wall. It was too loud and too frightening! And then the express train blew into the little local station and whooshed past without even stopping. The people at the edge of the platform just stood there as their coats flapped and the train sped by. Miki watched them, horrified. How could they stand there, so close to that roaring monster?

The noise seemed to hang in the air, even after the train was gone and Miki had dared to pull herself away from the wall. How could Emi and Ben have dared to climb onto that huge roaring thing? Miki was tempted to go home. She knew the way.

But she had come to get Emi. She was on one of those horrible loud things, and Miki was going to get her back.

Luckily, the next train was a local one, much slower and quieter as it rumbled toward the platform. It was so much less scary than the roaring express that Miki managed to come all the way out from under the bench as it pulled in. She flinched a little at the beeping of the doors, but she was sure she remembered that noise from when Emi and Ben had gotten off the train before.

But there were so many doors.... Miki stood next to a man with a pile of suitcases and watched anxiously as people got off the train. Quite a few of them smiled at her, thinking that she belonged to the suitcase man, or the girl with the headphones standing next to him and not realizing that no one was holding the little dog's leash.

None of these people was Ben or Emi. Miki whined anxiously. Now the people were all walking away down the platform. The man with the suitcases was picking them up and getting onto the train, and so was the girl.

Where was Emi? Miki barked, trying to tell Emi she was here, waiting, but all that happened was a man in a dark uniform at the end of the platform turned around and shouted something. He started to walk toward her, looking angry, and then the beeping noise sounded again.

Miki whimpered, feeling frightened. Emi must still be on the train—maybe Emi just hadn't seen her.

Panicking, Miki jumped onto the

train just as the doors began to slide closed. She jumped so fast that she skidded across the floor, sliding into the corner on the other side of the train and landing winded against the opposite doors. She sat there, gasping with fear, as the train pulled away.

After a couple of minutes, Miki sat up straighter. Being in a train didn't feel that much different than the car. And she could move around, since she wasn't in her little travel cage. She would go and look for Emi. She had to be here somewhere.

The shouting man had scared her, so Miki didn't want to walk down the aisle between the seats in case anybody else shouted at her like that. She would go quietly, she decided, and try not to let anyone see her. She whipped around the little wall by the doors and quickly edged under the first set of seats. The train was mostly empty, and she could dart from hiding space to hiding space, occasionally hurrying across the aisle to avoid a set of feet. Every time she stopped, she would look hopefully for Emi and Ben, but they were never there.

She was almost at the end of the train car when she stopped under an empty table. There was a delicious smell of food, and Miki was hungry. She sat and looked out at the seats across the aisle. A mother was sitting there with a baby and a little boy. The boy was eating a sandwich.

It smelled like ham, and Miki watched him enviously. It smelled so good that she was drooling.

The mother was pointing out the window, showing the baby the view. She wasn't looking at Miki at all. But the little boy seemed to feel Miki's hungry eyes fixed on his food. He leaned over, peering under the table, and then he smiled.

Miki gave him a hopeful Shiba smile back—open mouth, tongue hanging out a little. With her dark mouth against the golden fur of her muzzle, it really did look as though she was smiling. The little boy giggled and tore off a piece of his sandwich, holding it out to her.

"Hello!" he whispered.

Miki squirmed closer, crossing the aisle, and gratefully nibbled the sandwich out of his hand. He patted her delightedly, and Miki rubbed her head against his hand. It was so nice to have someone pay attention to her.

"Alex, what are you doing?"

Miki scurried back under the seats behind the table. The little boy's mom sounded angry.

"There was a dog! I gave him some of my sandwich. He was hungry."

"Alex, there isn't a dog. Don't be silly. Eat your sandwich, please."

"There is, look! Look, Mommy! He's under the table!"

Miki wriggled back farther as the mother leaned over to look, too.

"Alex, there really isn't! Just eat your lunch!"

The little boy said nothing back, but a minute or so later, Miki saw a hand come down past one of the nearby seats with the other half of the sandwich and a piece of cheese. He dropped them carefully under his seat and then he waved at Miki, obviously trying to show the puppy that they were there.

Miki sneaked carefully across the gangway and tucked herself away under the boy's seat, wolfing down the food. Then she gently pushed her cold nose against the boy's ankle to say thank you.

"Dad...."

"Mmmm?"

"Can I call Mom? Just to check if Miki's okay? She's not used to us being away longer than a weekend."

"Of course you can. I was just going to make some sandwiches for lunch. Then maybe this afternoon we could go and look at the shops downtown."

Emi nodded. Dad was trying really

hard to keep them both happy. It was tricky sometimes, especially with the two of them liking different things.

"Thanks, Dad." She gave him a hug as she went to pick up the phone. She would call Mom's cell phone, just in case she was out.

The phone rang and rang, and Emi grinned, imagining Mom searching through her pockets for it. It was always in the last pocket she checked, or buried at the bottom of her pocketbook. Mom said she was sure it moved by itself.

"Hello?"

"It's me. Hi, Mom!"

"Oh, Emi! Is everything all right?"

"Yes, it's fine. I just wanted to check that Miki was okay. Not missing us too much. Are you okay, Mom? You sound stressed."

There was a brief silence on the other end of the line, and Emi's eyes widened. There was something wrong, she could tell.

"Mom, what is it?"

She heard Mom sigh and saw Dad coming toward her across the living room, looking worried.

"Emi, it's Miki. I fell on the ice and accidentally let go of her leash. She ran off, and now I can't find her. I've been everywhere for the last hour. Home, the park, back home again. I've asked all the people I've gone past, but no one's seen her. I just don't know where she could be!"

Chapter Seven
Trapped!

"Alex, come on. It's time to get off."

"But Mommy, the dog.... He's still there."

"There isn't a dog, Alex. I checked," the woman said as she zipped up the baby's snowsuit. "Come on. Everyone else is off the train already. If there was a dog, he would have gone with his owner, wouldn't he? This is the last

stop. The dog is going home, too."

Miki saw the little boy lean down, peering under the seats. She almost wriggled further out to see him, but then a man in a dark uniform came hurrying down the aisle, and she stayed hidden. She remembered that other man on the station platform shouting at her.

The little boy followed his mother off the train, still looking around every so often. "Bye, dog!" he whispered as he stepped off.

Miki poked her nose out from under the seats and looked up and down. No one else was left. The man was gone, and the train was empty. Maybe she should get off, like the little boy. The train had stopped a couple of times before, but then only for a minute or so, and more people had gotten on. This seemed different.

She crept out into the aisle and went to look out the doors. It was cold out there and starting to get dark. The station looked as empty as the train, and it didn't seem familiar at all. For some reason, Miki had thought she would be back where she had started, but this was a completely different place. And where was Emi? This was all wrong! She had come to find her owner, and instead she had just gotten herself lost.

Miki whimpered and peered out at the station, the lights bright and yellowish in the gray of the winter afternoon. Maybe she had better get out and look for Emi. After all, Emi definitely wasn't on this train, so there was no point staying here.

Just as she made the decision and stepped forward, the doors beeped suddenly and then slid shut with a thump.

She was trapped.

"Emi, don't panic. It'll be all right—
we'll find her," said Dad.

"But Mom said she's asked everyone!
She says she doesn't know where Miki
is!" Emi gasped. She turned to her
brother, who looked equally worried.

"Well, we'll go and help her look,
then," said Dad. "Come on. You were
going back tomorrow morning anyway,
and you're not going to have a good time
here this afternoon when you're worrying
about Miki. I'll come with you, and we'll
all search for her. We'll take the train
back, since it's a lot quicker than going in
the car. Please pass me the phone, Emi.
I'll call your mom and explain. Go and
pack up your stuff. And don't forget to

look in the bathroom!" Dad called after her, but Emi had already disappeared to find all her things.

It was the fastest packing she and Ben had ever managed, and they were ready to go only 10 minutes later. Dad had checked the schedule, and he said there was a train very soon, but he wasn't sure they'd make it, with the walk to the station, too. Emi was determined that they would, though. She didn't care that there was another train not long after. She wanted to get back home at once.

Miki sat by the train doors, whining. What was she going to do now? The lights had gone off when the doors slid shut, and she was all alone in the dark train. She could still see, of course, but the train felt odd in the dark—too quiet. She didn't understand what was happening. Emi was supposed to have been on the train, and now she had lost everybody, even Mom.

Miki lay down next to the doors, resting her nose on her paws and whimpering miserably. What if she was stuck here?

Then a sudden beeping noise made her sit up. The doors! The doors made a noise like that! Miki looked up, but the doors didn't move. The noise was from farther down the train.

She got up and went to look. A lady had opened a set of doors at the other end of the train car and climbed on with a big black bag. The lights came on again, and Miki watched as the lady closed the doors and then moved down the train, humming to herself and picking up all the garbage that had been left behind.

Miki didn't care if the lady saw her or was angry. She just wanted to get off the train now. The puppy padded down the aisle toward the lady and then stood next to her and barked.

The cleaning lady had earphones in, and she was humming along to her music. She only half heard the bark, and then she looked down and noticed a dog right next to her—a dog that had appeared out of nowhere.

The lady was so shocked that she dropped the garbage bag. She didn't like dogs all that much, especially when they crept up on her. She darted down the aisle and unlocked the doors, hurrying off the train to catch her breath and tell one of the platform staff that there was a fierce dog on the train and it had tried to bite her.

Miki stared after the lady in surprise. She had no idea why she had run away. But she had left the doors open, and that was what mattered. Miki raced forward and jumped off the train at once, before they could shut on her again.

She stood on the empty platform, looking around uncertainly. Where should she go? Could Emi be here somewhere? Wearily, she walked along the platform, avoiding the patches of snow, and started to climb the steps at the end. She didn't really know where she was going. But Emi definitely wasn't on that train, so she would just have to keep looking.

She padded along the tunnel-like footbridge to the other platform and then looked worriedly at the steps on the other side. They were steep, not like the stairs at home. She was used to those now, and she could run up and down them without thinking. These steps were metal and open at the back, and they looked slippery. Miki picked her way down them carefully, wishing her leash wasn't dangling down. It kept getting tangled in her paws.

At the bottom of the steps was a ticket office and a waiting room, which looked warm and bright. But its glass door was tightly closed against the cold, and Miki couldn't see how to get in. She sniffed at the door sadly and then trailed past, looking out at the busy road that ran in front of the station.

A tall man came hurrying in, glancing up at the clock outside the ticket office. He didn't see Miki, but he tripped over her leash. He yelled as he almost fell over in the grayish snow that had been brushed to the side of the walkway.

Miki didn't stay to be shouted at again. First the man in uniform at the other station, then the lady with the

garbage bag, and now this. Mom and Emi and Ben didn't shout at her—except the time that she'd chewed Ben's sneakers, and then Emi had given her a hug, even though Ben was angry. She scurried around the corner of the building and hid behind a ticket machine. There was a little gap there, just wide enough for a very small dog. She would stay there and wait for Emi, out of the cold wind.

Miki wriggled herself comfortable—as comfortable as she could—and peered out, watching the people arrive for the next train.

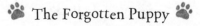

But the thud of feet and the muttering of the announcements blurred together, and she rested her nose on her paws and fell asleep.

Chapter Eight
A Lucky Break

"Dad, run!"

"Emi, honestly, we won't get to it in time. I've got to buy my ticket, remember? Don't worry. There's another train not long after." He pulled out his wallet and started to tap the screen on the ticket machine.

"It's still there…," Emi pleaded, looking up at the departures board.

"Couldn't we try? It's so cold now, and it's starting to snow again. I hate thinking of Miki outside in this weather, all on her own. Oh, it's almost leaving! Couldn't we go and wait by it and just say that you're coming in a minute?" She gazed across to the other platform, watching the train.

Ben gave her a hug. "It's only 15 minutes until the next one, Emi. We'll get home and find her. It'll be all right."

"But what if we don't?" Emi said miserably. "What if we've lost Miki forever?"

Ben shook his head. "I bet she hasn't gone far. I know Mom has looked for her, but Miki is probably scared being out on her own, that's all. She's not used to it. She's hiding somewhere really close to home, and she'll come out when she's feeling less frightened, and we'll find her."

Dad pulled his ticket out of the machine.

"Is it still there? Come on, let's run!" cried Emi. "We've got to find Miki!"

Miki twitched in her dream, thinking that she could hear Emi calling her name. Then she sprang up, shaking her head.

She *had* heard Emi! Emi was close by!

Miki stuck her nose out from behind the ticket machine, looking around desperately. She was still a little dazed from her cold sleep, but she could see the train on the other side of the station. Could Emi be on it?

Miki darted out, yapping, calling to Emi to stop, to wait for her. But as she tried to run, something dragged at her, pulling her back.

Her leash was caught! Miki whined

out loud—Emi was just over there, she was sure of it. She had found Emi at last, and now she couldn't reach her!

"My goodness, what's the matter? Are you lost?" An elderly lady was standing next to her, looking down at her worriedly. "Poor little thing."

Miki ignored the lady, pulling again at her leash. She had to catch Emi!

"Oh, you're stuck. Stand still, silly thing. There." She reached over and unhooked the leash from the piece of broken brick it was caught on. "Now, who do you belong to? Oh!"

Miki was gone, not even stopping to let the lady pet her. She was scrambling up the slippery metal steps and racing across the footbridge.

But when she got to the top of the steps, the train was gone. She could just see it in the distance. She had lost Emi again! Miki sat down at the top of the steps and howled and howled.

"We were so close!" Emi sat down on the bench in the little waiting room and put her hands over her eyes. She knew it was silly to cry about missing a train, but every minute mattered. What if Miki was hiding somewhere, just waiting for Emi to come and find her?

Ben made a face. "I know—I think they could have waited, honestly. Thirty seconds earlier and we would have caught it. What is *that*?"

A high-pitched yowling was echoing across the station, and all three of them peered out the waiting-room windows, trying to see where it was coming from.

"It sounds like a cross between a police car and a baby," Dad said, smiling a little. "That is one miserable dog. Oh, Emi, don't be sad. I'm sure there's nothing wrong with him—it's probably waiting in a car outside the station, that's all."

"It sounds like Miki when we leave her behind!" Emi whispered, getting to her feet. "But it can't be...."

"It does sound like her," Ben said, nodding.

"Really?" Dad frowned. "It seems unlikely…. She couldn't have followed you onto a train, could she?"

Emi and Ben exchanged doubtful glances. "Well, she has been to the station a few times to see us off. But she wouldn't get on a train…."

"I bet she would," Ben said. "If she thought you were on it, Emi. You know she misses you a ton."

"It *is* Miki…," Emi said, running to the door as a particularly loud wail echoed across the station. "It sounds just like her. It is!"

She darted out onto the platform, looking around wildly. And there, up at the top of the stairs, was a little dog, with her head lifted up, howling in misery.

"Miki!" Emi screamed, and Miki stopped mid-howl and stared.

Emi hadn't left after all. Emi was right there! Barking joyfully, Miki hurled herself down the stairs and into Emi's arms.

"You know, if we hadn't missed that train, we might never have found her," Emi said thoughtfully, looking at Miki sitting next to her on the platform. "I think about it every time I get on a train now."

It was several months later, and Emi and Ben were with their dad at the station. But this time it wasn't because they were going home—they were going on vacation!

Dad smiled at her. "Aren't you glad I was so slow getting my ticket that day? By the way, do you have your ticket, Emi? And all your bags? I really don't want to miss this train."

Emi looked down at the bags by her feet and counted them hurriedly.

"No, it's all right. I've got everything. I thought for a minute that I didn't have Miki's bag, with her bed and her bowls and all her toys, but I have it."

"That dog has more luggage than you and Ben," Dad said, grinning.

"Thanks for letting her come on vacation with us, Dad." Emi put an arm around his waist. "It's going to be wonderful, taking her to the beach and watching her run along the sand. Oooh, the train's coming!"

Miki stood up, looking at the train suspiciously. It was the first time she had seen one of those huge, loud things since Emi and Ben and Dad had brought her home. She still didn't like trains very much. She hated going to the station to say good-bye to Emi. Though at least now she knew that Emi wasn't gone forever— she would always come back.

But this time it was different. Emi was holding her leash and her bed was in a bag—Miki could smell it—just next to them. Miki was almost sure that she was getting on this train, too.

"Are you ready, Miki?" Emi whispered. "We're all going on a trip together."

Miki squashed herself tightly up against Emi's leg as the train pulled in and everyone picked up their bags.

She was not going to let Emi get lost again....

HOLLY WEBB

Holly Webb started out as a children's book editor, and wrote her first series for the publisher she worked for. She has been writing ever since, with more than 100 books to her name. Holly lives in England with her husband, three young sons, and several cats who are always nosing around when she is trying to type on her laptop.

For more information
about Holly Webb visit:

www.holly-webb.com
www.tigertalesbooks.com